THE GHASTLY McNASTYS

FRIGHT IN THE NIGHT

THE GHASTLY MCNASTYS

FRIGHT IN THE NIGHT

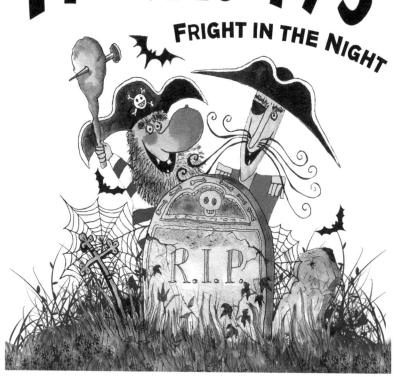

R.I.P.

Lyn Gardner • Ros Asquith

KIDS CAN PRESS

For Captain KJG — L.G.

For Lola, Lenny and Lucille — R.A.

This edition published by Kids Can Press in 2016

First published in the UK by Piccadilly Press

Text © 2014 Lyn Gardner
Illustrations © 2014 Ros Asquith

Kids Can Press acknowledges the financial support of the Government of Ontario, through the Ontario Media Development Corporation's Ontario Book Initiative.

Published in Canada by	Published in the U.S. by
Kids Can Press Ltd.	Kids Can Press Ltd.
25 Dockside Drive	2250 Military Road
Toronto, ON M5A 0B5	Tonawanda, NY 14150

www.kidscanpress.com

The text is set in Bembo Std.

Kids Can Press edition:
Edited by Katie Scott
Designed by Michael Reis

The hardcover edition of this book is smyth sewn casebound.
The paperback edition of this book is limp sewn with a drawn-on cover.

Manufactured in Malaysia in 9/2015 by Tien Wah Press (Pte.) Ltd.

CM 16 0 9 8 7 6 5 4 3 2 1
CM PA 16 0 9 8 7 6 5 4 3 2 1

Library and Archives Canada Cataloguing in Publication

Gardner, Lyn, author
    The Ghastly McNastys : fright in the night / written by Lyn Gardner ; illustrated by Ros Asquith.

(The Ghastly McNastys ; 3)
Originally published: London : Piccadilly Press, 2014.
ISBN 978-1-77138-130-7 (bound) — ISBN 978-1-77138-148-2 (pbk.)

    I. Asquith, Ros, illustrator II. Title.

PZ7.G1765Ghf 2016   j823'.92   C2015-902966-X

Kids Can Press is a *lorus*™ Entertainment company

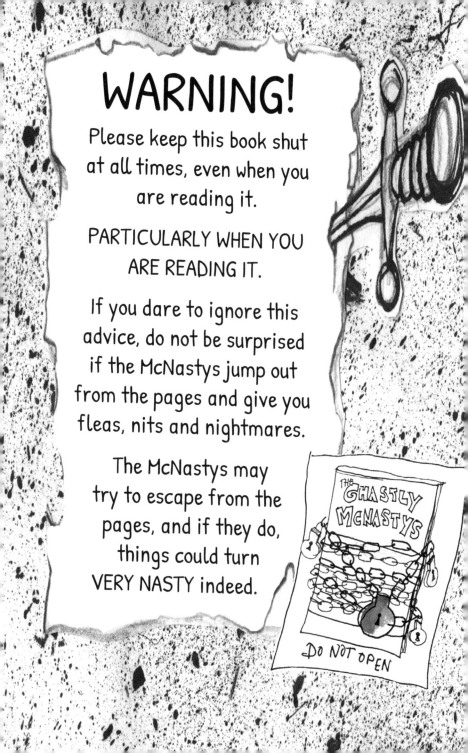

WARNING!

Please keep this book shut at all times, even when you are reading it.

PARTICULARLY WHEN YOU ARE READING IT.

If you dare to ignore this advice, do not be surprised if the McNastys jump out from the pages and give you fleas, nits and nightmares.

The McNastys may try to escape from the pages, and if they do, things could turn VERY NASTY indeed.

THE GHASTLY McNASTYS

DO NOT OPEN

Chapter 342

(Do not be utterly ridiculous. You cannot begin a book with Chapter 342, as this would be very confusing for everyone and like starting the alphabet with *N* or eating pizza and strawberry ice cream for breakfast.)

Chapter 1

Jamie Fried-Trout, the cabin boy, was standing high up in the crow's nest on the mast of the fishing trawler *The Good Hope*. He had been chosen as a lookout because he was the only member of the crew who was fit enough to climb up to the crow's nest. But he was not an ideal choice because he suffered from terrible

The Good Hope

seasickness and was always too busy shouting, "Oops, sorry!" to all those he was being sick over on the deck below to notice anything on the horizon.

Since Jamie had been lookout, *The Good Hope* had sailed into the world's biggest iceberg (which immediately melted in shock, causing sea levels to rise dangerously), collided with Australia (which had shifted several hundred feet to the right) and hit Canada (which now had a terrible dent in it). Jamie had been obliged to say, "Oops, sorry!" a lot recently.

Worst of all had been the giant squid, whose tentacles had gotten completely knotted after *The Good Hope* ran into it.

Jamie had apologized profusely and promised that he would never eat calamari again (not even when it is grilled with garlic, lemon juice and olive oil, which is scrumptious). But the giant squid was in no mood for apologies. When it eventually untied itself, it waved its tentacles like a fist at Jamie and swam away with revenge so clearly glinting in its eye that Jamie began to wish that his parents had never met.

How he longed to be back on dry land, preferably in Little Snoring with his cousin Trevor Augustus Trout, otherwise known as Tat, and Tat's best friend, Hetty. Hetty was the cleverest girl in the world and would surely know how to cure seasickness and placate a vengeful squid. She knew everything. Well, almost everything, since she didn't know that guinea pigs yawn to show anger or that fleas can survive for over a year without eating. She also didn't know where Captain Syd's lost treasure was buried in Little Snoring.

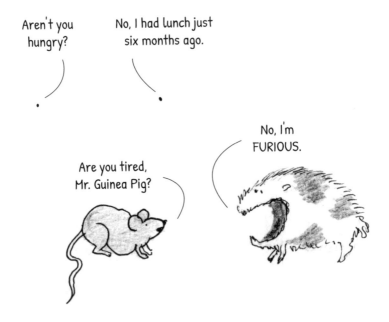

But she and Tat were working on finding the treasure with the help of the treasure map, which had been found in the ancient Little Snoring Castle. Jamie was going to help them.

Jamie knew that it was essential for them to find the treasure as soon as possible because Tat had told him that, as usual, the Trout family finances were in a very unfortunate state. Every time Mrs. Trout tried to make ends meet, the ends wriggled farther apart like over-excitable worms. Mrs. Trout had taken on an extra part-time job at the local café, and Mr. Trout was trying to invent things, hoping to add to his meager earnings as Little Snoring's lighthouse keeper. So far he had invented the wheel, electricity, ice cream and glow-in-the-dark paint and had been very disappointed to discover that somebody had already invented them all.

He was now working on a top-secret new invention. Tat had told Jamie he thought it had something to do with glue.

The ship had been due to dock in Little Snoring a few days earlier and was already late because of bad weather. Jamie was worried they might not arrive in time for the Little Snoring Junior Costume Dance. He already had his costume made and had hidden it under his bunk in his cabin. He was planning to go as the vengeful ghost of Captain Syd. He hoped to scare everyone witless.

But before they reached Little Snoring, he was hopeful that he might redeem himself with *The Good Hope*'s crew. So when he heard a strange noise coming from somewhere out at sea, he tried to forget his queasy belly and be as alert as possible.

He looked through the telescope and saw a shark zigzagging its way across the ocean toward the ship. The shark appeared to be in some distress, but the really odd thing was the noises coming from it. Jamie listened hard. There was no doubt—he could hear it clearly.

Sweaty socks!

Squeaky underpants!

This was no ordinary shark — it was a talking shark. It was also hiccuping very loudly.

"Talking, hiccuping shark, ahoy!" shouted Jamie. The captain of the trawler was so surprised that Jamie had spotted anything at all that she put the brakes on a bit too hard and the boat skidded so sharply to the left that everyone fell except Jamie, who was clinging to the mast very tightly.

The whole crew counted to ten, because in the hold they had a small cargo of dynamite that they were transporting to the Greater Snoring quarry, which was run by the trawler skipper's brother. But there was no explosion and everyone heaved a sigh of relief. Jamie clambered down the mast and joined the captain and the rest of the crew, who were rubbing their squashed noses and staring over the side of the boat at the shark. There, a strange sight met their eyes.

DYNAMITE

Turn off engine.
No mobile phones.
No matches or
silly business.
Flammable.
Handle with care.
Don't say you
were't warned.
This is not a toy.

Chapter 2

(Two is too, too good and twice as good as one,
which is often badly behaved and has to be
glued to the pages to make it stay.)

Sharks are very hard to catch (not that *The Good Hope* ever tried, since it was a specialist fishing vessel and only ever caught fish fingers). But the shark they were looking at kept rising up out of the sea and putting its flippers together as if it was begging to be let aboard.

What's more, it was clearly talking. Every time

it opened its mouth, the words "Sweaty socks!" and "Squeaky underpants!" could be heard. Its hiccups were getting worse, too, and its eyes more desperate.

HICCUP!

"Bring out the nets," shouted the captain. It was not often that she felt sorry for a shark, but this one was clearly in terrible distress and needed help.

The sailors threw the net overboard, the shark jumped in and everyone hauled it over the side of the boat and onto the deck, where it fell with a great big thud.

"Ouch!" said two voices inside the shark. The shark nodded desperately toward the captain's knife, which was secured in her belt. Reluctantly, the captain took out her knife, ready to cut down the middle of the shark's belly. She looked into the shark's eyes. The shark nodded again.

"Wait!" shouted Jamie. He remembered that when he had terrible hiccups or a stomachache he would sometimes feel better if his mom rubbed his back very hard. He ran over to the shark, motioned to the other sailors to help him turn it on its front and began to rub and pat the shark's back. The shark's hiccuping grew louder, and Jamie patted harder. Then all of a sudden it gave an enormous *BURRRP* (louder than a 10 000-ton meteor hitting the earth) and opened its mouth very wide. Two strange, smelly, misshapen creatures slithered out of the shark's mouth and onto the deck.

"Sweaty socks!" groaned one.

"Squeaky underpants!" moaned the other.

The stench coming from the creatures was unbearable, like maggoty fish mixed with your big brother's smelly socks that have been left in a corner of the bedroom since last spring.

"Poor shark!" said the captain. "It must have accidentally swallowed these repulsive, repellent sea monsters."

The two revolting creatures gave a shriek of anger and rose to their feet.

"I'm not repulsive! I am Captain Gruesome, and millions of people across the world consider me extraordinarily attractive, except I haven't met any of them yet," said one, snatching the captain's knife and waving it threateningly.

"How dare you call me repellent! I'm Captain Grisly. I'm proud that so many admire me and I declare that I am as handsome as a wombat, as cunning as a crocodile and as ferocious as a Tasmanian devil."

"And as smelly as a skunk," remarked the trawler captain, which was brave, but rather foolish. The McNastys advanced toward her so threateningly that even the sun was scared and hid behind a cloud.

"You won't be making any rude personal remarks when you are walking the plank," cackled Captain Gruesome, who was delighted to be released from the shark's belly and even happier that the opportunity to be ghastly and nasty had presented itself so soon.

He signaled to his brother, Grisly, who had found a suitable plank and secured it in place. The 423 fleas, two million nits, hundreds of mice and a ferret that had been living in Grisly's revolting, bushy beard immediately rushed toward the plank. They just couldn't wait to get away from him. If you listened hard, you could hear the tiniest of plops as each nit hit the sea.

"You next," said Grisly to the shark, which

shook its head at such stupidity and
looked at him with utter contempt as it
leaped overboard.

One by one, with Captain Gruesome
using his knife to tickle their backs
(which none of them found in the slightest
bit funny), the trawler captain and crew
were made to walk the plank. They went
SPLISH, SPLASH, SPLOSH or SPLAT as
they hit the water, depending on whether
they were tall or small.

"With any luck that nasty shark will be
waiting to gobble them all up," said Captain
Gruesome, grinning happily at the thought.

Jamie was at the very back of the line,

which was moving much faster than he would have liked. He couldn't swim — although he could put his head underwater in the bath and hold his breath for a very long time. And it was far too late to sign up for swimming lessons now.

Like the others before him, Jamie was forced onto the plank at knifepoint, and he began to shuffle toward the end and oblivion. (Oblivion is the place always found at the end of a plank suspended over shark-infested waters, and it has the postal code TH3 END. My pet terrapin was very keen that I should tell you this just in case you ever want to send a postcard to someone there. But do not expect to get a reply.)

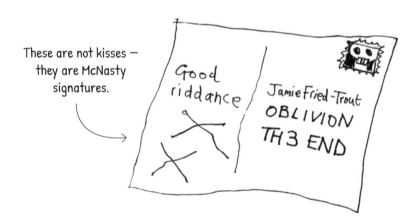

These are not kisses — they are McNasty signatures.

Good riddance

Jamie Fried-Trout
OBLIVION
TH3 END

Jamie realized that with his next step he would walk into thin air and plunge to his doom (like oblivion but nastier, and smelling of cat pee), when he felt himself being pulled back by the scruff of his neck.

"Hang on! We're going to need a cabin boy to boss around and be ghastly and nasty to on a regular basis, and you'll do, you revolting little pest," said Captain Gruesome. "Here, take this," he said, reaching in his pocket and pulling out a pirate flag. "Climb up the mast, and raise the skull and crossbones." He gave Jamie a kick on the bum, and the boy began to climb upward holding the flag.

Don't look down ...
Don't look down ...
Don't look down ...

Rotten Apple II

"Sweaty socks," cried Captain Gruesome happily as he found some cans of paint and leaned over the side of the boat. He began to paint over the name *The Good Hope* and replace it with *The Rotten Apple II.* "We're in command of our own ship again at last!"

"And where are we going to sail her?" asked Captain Grisly.

"Don't be a birdbrain, Grisly. There is only one place on earth we want to be: Little Snoring. That's where Captain Syd's lost treasure is just waiting for us to find it. Soon it will be all ours."

"Provided those horrible children Tat and Hetty, that hideous cat called Dog and that treacherous parrot called Polly haven't found it and stolen it all first," said Captain Grisly.

"Sweaty socks, we must hurry! Full speed ahead."

Both brothers rushed to take control of the wheel, and neither would let go, so they began to whack and wallop each other. Captain Grisly had realeased the ship's hand brake, and Captain

Gruesome had turned on the engine. The ship began to spin round and round in circles.

Up in the crow's nest, Jamie hung on for dear life. In the distance he could just see the shark swimming along with the entire crew clinging to her tail. It was heading for a small island.

The spinning was beginning to make Jamie feel very queasy. He leaned out of the crow's nest and vomited with perfect accuracy all over the Ghastly McNastys below. "Oops, sorry!" he cried.

The McNastys shook their fists and shouted at him to put up the pirate flag and then come down immediately. Jamie shook his head. He was too loyal to dream of flying any pirate flag on *The Good Hope*, and he definitely wasn't going to take orders from the McNastys. Jamie stuffed the pirate flag in his pocket and decided it was safest to stay where he was, up in the crow's nest, out of the pirates' reach.

Chapter 3

(Crowded with excitement.)

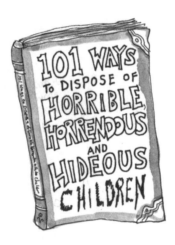

The Ghastly McNastys gazed upward and were rewarded by a low-flying seagull pooping all over their noses.

Yet again, the pirates shook their fists at Jamie Fried-Trout and shouted for him to come down. And yet again, Jamie ignored them and took another swig from the large water bottle that he kept in the crow's nest. Then he took a bite from one of the jam sandwiches that, like his cousin, he always kept in his pocket for emergencies such as being kidnapped by pirates.

Jamie was only a few feet away at the top of the mast, but as far as the McNastys were concerned, he could be on the moon or in Bigbottoms-by-the-Sea. He had ignored all the McNastys' attempts to lure him down for three whole days. The McNastys wished they had made

Jamie walk the plank with the others — by now he would have been fish food. They had tried shooting him with their catapults, but they had terrible aim and instead they had hit the moon with the dried snot balls they were using as ammunition and given the man in the moon a terrible headache.

The McNastys use snot balls in their catapults.

They had tried enticing Jamie down by smiling nicely (which was slightly more terrifying than being charged by rioting armored armadillos) and telling him they were going to give him lemonade and chocolate cake (which they weren't, because they had already guzzled all the lemonade and eaten all the chocolate cake that they had found in the hold alongside several sticks of dynamite).

Now they had arrived in a secluded cove near Little Snoring, so getting Jamie down was a matter of urgency.

"Sweaty socks," said Captain Gruesome, "that boy is as stubborn as a mule and twice as ugly. Though not quite as furry."

"Squeaky underpants," said Captain Grisly. "We will have to starve him out."

"We don't have time. He's got his own water and sandwiches. It could be weeks before he falls off his perch from lack of food and drink, and by then those revolting children and that nasty cat called Dog and that treacherous parrot will have found the treasure. Have another look in the book in case there is a suggestion that we've missed."

Captain Grisly turned the pages of a well-thumbed copy of *101 Ways to Dispose of Horrible, Horrendous and Hideous Children*, which they had borrowed from the Captain Bluebeard Memorial Library and had never taken back. They now owed $433.26 in fines and they had no intention of paying any of it.

The book offered excellent advice on boiling children in vats of oil, poisoning them with Truly Scrumptious, Perfectly Poisonous Jam Sandwich Flavored Fudge, throwing them into pits full of angry vipers or putting them through a mincer and transforming them into frosted sugary icing for cupcakes. Grisly thought the iced cupcakes sounded very tasty. But while the recipe began with "1. Catch your child …" it gave no advice at all about how to do so.

If the fine hadn't been so much, Captain Grisly would have taken the book back to the library and complained very loudly about the uselessness of the books they lent, and in revenge blocked out the words *and*, *the*, *hippopotamus* and *happy* in all the other library books.

The McNastys were beginning to feel quite sorry for themselves. They had escaped from the belly of the shark and hijacked *The Good Hope*. They had sailed the boat around the island of Little Snoring, far enough away not to be spotted, and they had put down anchor in an isolated cove on the uninhabited side of the island.

It had all passed without incident if you ignored the fact that every time they came on deck, Jamie was sick all over them. (The McNastys began to suspect he was using them as target practice.) Oh, and there was their unfortunate run-in with a giant squid when they recklessly steered the boat into it, even though Jamie had shouted, "Look out! Giant squid!" very loudly several times. Jamie apologized profusely to the squid, but the McNastys just laughed very rudely. As the squid untangled itself and swam away, they shouted after it, "Boo hoo. Armed but not very dangerous."

They regretted it because the squid turned back and sprayed both of them with thick black ink. Jamie clapped and cheered, and both the McNastys had to take baths, which they hated since they had to look at themselves in the bathroom mirror, which always gave them a terrible fright. Having seen the McNastys' encounter with the squid, Jamie felt quite confident that he was no longer at the top of the giant squid's most wanted list.

WANTED

FOR CRIMES AGAINST SQUID

Katie Kipper

For discriminating against those with multiple limbs.

Barry Bloater

For squid battering and deep frying.

Gruesome & Grisly McNasty

For all of the above, plus nose-picking, belching, stealing toys, stomping on toddlers, etc., etc. (Full list runs to 6004 pages.)

Jamie Fried-Trout

For vomit pollution.

Now the McNastys knew (and unlike Hetty they seldom knew anything) that all they had to do was find out where Tat and Hetty were digging for treasure, wait until the children found it and then steal it for themselves.

But their dastardly plan was going wrong. If they left Jamie up the mast, what was to stop him from swimming ashore as soon as they had left and raising the alarm? They had to get him down and deal with him.

The McNastys could wait no longer. Even now they feared that Tat and Hetty were uncovering diamonds and counting gold doubloons, and taking it all to the bank for safekeeping. They had to get to Little Snoring as quickly as possible.

Captain Gruesome picked up an ax and swung the head hard against the mast. Captain Grisly picked up another ax and took aim, too.

"Sweaty socks! This is hard work," said Gruesome, whose idea of hard work was lying in a hammock eating ice-cream sundaes.

"Squeaky underpants! This is exhausting," said Grisly, who was as lazy as a three-toed sloth and sometimes found putting on his socks in the morning so exhausting that he gave up bothering and just went back to bed.

It took ages, but eventually they managed to cut their way through the wooden mast.

"Timber!" shouted Gruesome as the mast toppled down, narrowly avoiding crushing the McNastys as flat as (please choose your own answer):

A) Pancakes

B) Holland

C) An elephant after it has been run over by a steamroller

(No elephants were harmed in the making of this page.)

The mast fell so that its top end, where Jamie was holding on for dear life, was over the edge of the boat. For a moment Jamie clung on to it, his feet dangling over the sea below. But his fingers began to slip. The McNastys both raised their right hands and waved at him like a couple of kind uncles saying goodbye to a beloved nephew. They could see from Jamie's stricken face that he was losing the battle to hang on to the mast and they were thrilled.

"I can't swim!" he cried, hoping desperately that the McNastys would show mercy.

"Not our problem," said the McNastys, annoyed they had gone to so much unnecessary bother to cut down the mast. If they had known he couldn't swim, they could just have sunk the spare rowboat and left him stranded on the ship.

"Bye-bye, dear boy," said Captain Gruesome sweetly.

"Adieu," said Captain Grisly, who always felt that speaking in French lent an elegance to every occasion, including those that involved the permanent disposal of small, irritating boys. Jamie knew that he could hold on no longer.

His fingers uncurled, his body dropped like a stone and he plunged into the sea and disappeared under the water. The McNastys ran to the side of the ship and peered over the edge. They waited and then they waited some more. There was no sign of Jamie. They high-fived each other.

"A job well done," said Gruesome. "The world will thank us for ridding it of another nasty, petulant, pesky child."

"They will probably give us a prize. Maybe even a medal — a very big solid-gold one encrusted with diamonds," said Grisly. "Let's lower one of the rowboats and head straight to Little Snoring."

And they did, but only after they had gone into the hold and removed some sticks of dynamite in case the children had already found the treasure and taken it to the bank and they needed to blast their way into the vaults.

Chapter 4

(Can be divided into quarters and read
one bit at a time if you prefer.)

Tat and Hetty were hot and tired. They had
spent the morning digging for treasure by the
cliffs, which were very close to the old abandoned
graveyard and at the point where the sparkling
silvery sands of the Little Snoring beach met the
Big, Scary, Very Dark, Dense Forest Where No
One In Their Right Mind Would Want To Go,

which had gotten BIGGER and SCARIER than it had been before. Few people did go there, so Tat and Hetty had been entirely undisturbed.

But Tat's heart wasn't in it. It was hard to get excited about treasure when he was so worried about the disappearance of *The Good Hope* and his cousin Jamie.

Dog, who although he was a cat behaved like a dog, had spent the morning digging for bones at the bottom of the cliff. Dog was helped by Pegleg Polly the parrot, who had once belonged to the McNastys but who had escaped when she realized they wanted to turn her into parrot burgers.

So far Tat and Hetty had found no sign of treasure, but Dog and Polly had found many bones, some of them rather large, which Dog thought were much more valuable than diamonds or gold coins. Dog didn't see the point of gold coins or diamonds, as trying to chew either of them would do your teeth no good at all.

Tat and Hetty were not disheartened about their lack of success so far: after studying the map that was found in the castle, they were certain that they were closer than they'd ever been to discovering Captain Syd's lost treasure.

Seeing her friend's sad face and hoping to cheer him up, Hetty said, "I'm sure tomorrow will be the day, but we won't tell anyone, except our families. We don't want anyone else finding the treasure before us. And who knows, maybe *The Good Hope* will be found and Jamie will be here to share our good fortune."

They didn't mind packing up early because it was the night of the Little Snoring Junior Costume Dance. Hetty and Tat were both going as skeletons and they needed to check their costumes. They had made them using some of the glow-in-the-dark paint that Tat's dad, Mr. Trout, had invented before he realized that somebody had already invented it. There were cans of it in the garden shed.

On their way home, Hetty and Tat stopped off at the village shop to buy the fish fingers that Tat's dad, Mr. Trout, had asked them to get for dinner.

Dog and Pegleg Polly waited patiently outside. Dog started falling asleep and dreaming of gnawing a leg bone from a diplodocus. Dog frequently bit off more than he could chew, and a 150-million-year-old diplodocus bone would be quite something to chew on.

Pegleg Polly was being fed birdseed by Mrs. Slime, the McNastys' former second mate (regretful and reformed), who had just been to the shop to buy forty-two packets of tissues because she sneezed all the time.

"No fish fingers, I'm afraid," said Mrs. Groan, the village gossip, who ran the Little Snoring village

shop, an emporium of obscure discounted items
that nobody in their right mind would want to
buy but often resorted to in an emergency.

"There has been a high demand for them since
Monday when *The Good Hope* failed to dock in
the Little Snoring Harbor as expected. People
realized there might be a supply shortage. I could
rummage around in the freezer and see if I've got
any fish toes or fish elbows left, but they've never

been as popular as the fingers. Or I do have tarts filled with pickled herring and marshmallows (such a clever, time-saving idea to put a main course and dessert together in a single flaky pastry shell). Or I might be able to find the last jar of alligator and yaks' milk pâté; it has proved unexpectedly popular despite the fact it tends to bite the tongues of anyone who tries to eat it."

Hetty shuddered. Mrs. Groan shook her head sadly.

"It's a terrible thing about *The Good Hope*. Your cousin Jamie was on board, wasn't he, Tat?"

Tat nodded sadly.

There had been much speculation in the *Little Snoring Gazette* (never the most reliable of newspapers) as to what had happened to the fishing vessel, which had so mysteriously disappeared. On Tuesday the headlines proclaimed that it had sunk in a storm; on Wednesday that it had been attacked by a giant squid; and this morning the newspaper speculated that the boat had been blown to smithereens by the small cargo of dynamite it was ferrying to the Greater Snoring quarry as a favor to the trawler skipper's brother.

Tat didn't know what to think, but he wasn't going to give up hope until after the Little Snoring Junior Costume Dance that he and Jamie had gone to together every year for the last five years. He knew that if Jamie didn't turn up tonight, there was no hope. Jamie would never miss the Little Snoring Junior Costume Dance, not even if he was being chased by a hoard of hungry mutant zombie armadillos. He had won first prize for his costume for the last three years.

A man rushed into the shop. He was wearing a deerstalker hat and held a very large magnifying glass in one hand and a pair of handcuffs in the other. He peered very hard at Tat and Hetty through the magnifying glass as if studying them for clues. Tat found himself feeling guilty, even though he hadn't done anything wrong.

"Ah, Inspector Gullible Haddock, always on the job and looking for clues," simpered Mrs. Groan. "The Inspector," she told the children, "is in charge of the investigation into *The Good Hope*. He is completely tireless."

"I have left no stone unturned," said Inspector Haddock, who indeed only that morning had looked under more than 200 stones and had found no trace of *The Good Hope* but had found a great many woodlice, worms and a stag beetle, which had gripped his nose very hard with its pincers. He had come to the shop to buy a bandage.

"How are your investigations going?"

"I'm rooting out guilt everywhere I go, Mrs. Groan," said the Inspector, looking even harder at Tat and Hetty. "Already today I have arrested nine Scouts for helping old ladies cross the street without waiting for the green man at the traffic lights, and a woodchuck that kept chucking wood despite a very large sign forbidding it. Yesterday was an excellent day, too: I arrested three children for reading under the blankets with a flashlight after their parents told them to go to sleep, and thwarted some men who claimed to be mending a hole in the road but who I, with my advanced powers of deduction, realized were semi-hardened criminals attempting to steal a cement mixer."

"But what about your investigation into the disappearance of *The Good Hope*?" asked Tat. "Surely that's what you should be concentrating on?"

"Well, I don't want to boast," said Inspector Haddock, who enjoyed nothing more, "but I'm very good at juggling."

"Oh," said Mrs. Groan, "I had no idea that they taught circus skills in the police force."

Inspector Haddock glared at her, but wondered whether circus might be a useful skill to add to his armory of many talents, which already included getting the wrong end of the stick and barking up the wrong tree. (This does not mean that Inspector Haddock thought he was a dog, just that he was not very good at solving crimes.)

"My brain is so advanced that I can do several things at the same time. That's why the world's criminals quake with fear whenever they hear my name. I have not only been cracking down hard on the shocking lawlessness in Little Snoring but I've made a major breakthrough in the case of *The Good Hope*. I have discovered that *The Good Hope* was a victim of Captain Syd's ghostly curse. I believe that the vessel was abandoned by its crew and sank after the ghost of Captain Syd appeared on board the ship."

Inspector Haddock continued, "It is well known that Captain Syd's ghost is prone to make appearances when anyone gets close to discovering his lost treasure buried in Little Snoring. As *The Good Hope* was heading for Little Snoring Harbor, it could be that the ghost thought that the crew were looking for treasure. I have evidence: earlier in the week as I was walking home, I saw a strange glow and moving lights near the Big, Scary, Very Dark, Dense Forest Where No One In Their Right Mind Would Want To Go, which had gotten BIGGER and SCARIER than it had been before. I am quite certain it was the ghost of Captain Syd."

"Actually —" said Hetty, who was about to tell Inspector Haddock that what he had seen was unlikely to be a ghost and more likely to be her and Tat digging for treasure after dark. But Inspector Haddock raised a hand to stop her.

"Do not interrupt me, little girl. My investigation is almost complete. I shall be making an arrest very soon. As long as my force stops bothering me with stupid unrelated incidents such as the appearance of a shark in Little Snoring Harbor surrounded by a cloud of fleas and nits and with a ferret sitting on its back."

He shook his head and said wearily, "They are such buffoons. It is hard for me to put up with their stupidity. But I assure you, an arrest is imminent. As far as I'm concerned the case is solved and closed. I'm now concentrating all my energies on investigating the mysterious disappearance of two pairs of extra-large underpants and a quantity of ladies' clothing from a clothesline in Little Snoring this morning. I have a brain the size of a melon, so I should have this mystery solved before the day is done."

Hetty knew that nobody's brain could be the size of a melon because it would not fit inside your head, and if it did it would make your head so heavy it wouldn't stay upright on your neck.

She suppressed a loud snort. Tat glanced at his friend. She was clearly taking every word that Inspector Haddock was saying with a grain of salt. (This does not mean that Hetty had eaten 474 grains of salt — which is the exact number of words that Inspector Haddock has said so far, and please count if you don't believe me — as that would make her very thirsty and kill her. Taking something with a grain of salt is not like taking sugar with your tea. It means that you disbelieve everything that someone is saying.)

Tat wasn't so sure. Maybe there was something in Inspector Haddock's theory. After all, it was the policeman's job to investigate things.

Hetty turned to the policeman and asked sweetly, "Do tell me, Inspector, I'm very interested. How do you propose to go about arresting a ghost?"

Inspector Haddock frowned and then he said, "I cannot share my plans with you, little girl, but I assure you that I will outwit the spook. I have my handcuffs at the ready."

"I can't wait to see you make your arrest, Inspector," said Hetty politely and then she turned to Tat. "We've got to go. Your dad will be waiting for us."

"Sorry about the lack of fish fingers. I could offer a two-for-one deal on shepherds if your dad wants to make a shepherd's pie," said Mrs. Groan, who was always eager to make a sale.

"No, thank you," said Tat firmly. He didn't think it was kind to go around eating shepherds or very fair on sheep, which would all get lost and *baa* very miserably and keep everyone awake at night.

Fish use their fingers to cover their eyes when they see the McNastys.

"Or I've got a half-price toad only three weeks past its best-before date that comes with a free hole if you like toad in the hole," Mrs. Groan called after them. "Or I've got fishcakes but only with strawberry and licorice flavor buttercream icing …"

The children left the shop. Tat was very gloomy.

"I couldn't bear it if Jamie and the rest of the crew of *The Good Hope* were frightened to death by the ghost of Captain Syd."

"Oh, Tat," said Hetty. "Surely you don't believe in ghosts, do you?"

"Well," mumbled Tat, "I always think it's a good idea to keep an open mind about most things. What if Inspector Haddock's theory is right and the ghost of Captain Syd realizes we are close to finding his treasure and decides to come and get us next?"

"Come on, Tat, that policeman is completely clueless. If he thinks he can arrest a ghost, Inspector Gullible Haddock is even more stupid than his name suggests," she said. "I bet that our inspector wouldn't spot a clue even if it was right under his nose."

"What do you mean, Hetty?"

"Well, I've been thinking about that shark that the inspector mentioned turning up in Little Snoring Harbor in a cloud of fleas and nits and with a ferret sitting on its back. I've never heard of something like that happening before. I just wonder whether there might be a connection between the appearance of the shark and the disappearance of *The Good Hope* and all her crew, because both are very unusual occurrences."

Tat frowned. "Maybe it's just a coincidence, like lightning striking twice in the same place or Melancholy Smith, the fourth-grader, having a seagull poop on her head on the way to school every single morning for a week."

"Maybe you're right," said Hetty. "But when I think of fleas and nits, I also always think about the Ghastly McNastys, the nastiest and smelliest pirates ever to have sailed the seven seas. And when did we last see them? When they were swallowed by a shark."

Tat gasped. "Oh, Hetty, do you think the McNastys may have something to do with the disappearance of *The Good Hope*?"

"Yes," said Hetty. "I'm also interested in those missing underwear and women's clothes. I can't imagine how they are connected to the disappearance of *The Good Hope*, but it's another very unusual occurrence. I don't think Little Snoring has ever had a clothesline thief before. Unlike Inspector Haddock, we should keep all options and our eyes and ears open, and maybe we should do a bit of investigating

of our own and try to find out if the Ghastly
McNastys are responsible for the disappearance of
The Good Hope."

Chapter 5

Tat and Hetty, Tat's mom and dad and his little sister, Tallulah, scraped the last bit of food from their plates.

"That was scrumptious," said Mrs. Trout, looking anxiously at the kitchen clock. She didn't want to be late for her afternoon shift at the Little Snoring Café because it would be a busy one.

On Wednesday afternoons Mrs. Groan's shop was closed and anyone who wanted to hear the latest village gossip had to go to the café, which meant it was always full.

"You've got plenty of time, my dear," said Mr. Trout, "and we've got Baked Alaska for dessert." (This did not mean that the Trout family were planning to eat the forty-ninth state of the United States, which would be much too big for a small family like the Trouts to manage all on their own, and besides would never fit into their oven. Baked Alaska is a dessert made of cake piled high with ice cream, which is then smothered in meringue and baked in the oven at a high temperature for a short period of time. My terrapin says this is not cookery, but magic. I am inclined to agree.) "Have you got room?"

Mrs. Trout nodded. There is nobody in the world who hasn't got room for Baked Alaska, not even a mom in a hurry.

"Mrs. Trout," said Hetty, "would you mind if Tat and I accompanied you to the café?"

"Of course not, Hetty dear," said Mrs. Trout. "But I thought you and Tat were going to make your costumes this afternoon."

"We are," said Hetty, "but if I'm right and the McNastys are behind the disappearance of *The Good Hope* and are making their way to Little Snoring, they'll want to know exactly where Tat and I are digging for the treasure and how close we are to finding it. The café is the ideal place to spread a rumor around the village that the treasure is about to be found, particularly as Mrs. Groan always meets with her friends there on Wednesday afternoons. If the McNastys are hiding somewhere around, and they hear the rumor, it will make them take action."

"I'm a bit worried," said Mr. Trout with a frown. "It's an invitation for every criminal in Little Snoring to go down to the site of your dig and try to steal the treasure."

"Hetty and I thought about that," said Tat. "But as there are so few criminals in Little Snoring — except the ones that Inspector Haddock imagines — we thought we'd be pretty safe. And anyway, Inspector Haddock told Mrs. Groan that he knows for certain that the ghost of Captain Syd is responsible for the disappearance of *The Good Hope*, so that news will be all around the village by now. Mrs. Groan is such a gossip. People will be too frightened to go near the treasure site at night in case the ghost of Captain Syd really is on the loose and looking to take his revenge on anyone who tries to touch his treasure. The treasure site should be quite safe tonight, unless of course Inspector Haddock makes an arrest."

"Which we all know will never happen. You can't arrest a ghost," added Hetty. "That Inspector Haddock has fewer brains than a pickled herring. He's blind to the fact that the flea-infested shark, the ferret, fleas, nits and the missing underpants all suggest that Little Snoring's two most wanted criminals — the Ghastly McNastys — are on the loose."

"But if you are right, Hetty, and the McNastys have escaped from the shark's belly,

hijacked *The Good Hope* and made their way to
Little Snoring to grab Captain Syd's treasure, won't
they stay away from the treasure site tonight, too,
if they think there's a ghost about?" asked Tallulah.
"We know that they are such a pair of scaredy-cats.
If they're afraid of dentists and spiders, don't you
think they'll be really scared of ghosts, too?"

"Good question," said Hetty. "But if the McNastys were responsible for the disappearance of *The Good Hope*, they'll know that Inspector Haddock's theory about the ship being surprised by the ghost of Captain Syd is complete fishcakes. They'll see it as an opportunity to find and get their hands on the treasure without any interference. Anyway, the McNastys love treasure so much, nothing will put them off. Tat and I are banking on the fact that the lure of treasure will be too much for them to resist."

The McNastys loved treasure even more than they hated children.

"Yes," said Tat, "and when they turn up, Hetty and I will be waiting for them, and we'll find a way to make them tell us what happened to *The Good Hope*, and with any luck they will lead us to her and her crew."

Mrs. Trout shook her head. "It all sounds very dangerous to me. The McNastys are the nastiest and ghastliest pirates ever to have sailed the seven seas."

"Don't worry, my dear," said Mr. Trout, patting his wife's arm. "Have faith in Tat and Hetty. They've already outwitted the Ghasty McNastys twice before."

"Yes, but what if it's third time lucky for those horrible pirates?"

"We've got plenty of help," said Tat. "We've got Dog and Polly on our side." Dog wagged his tail enthusiastically, and Polly flew around the room squawking.

"And Mrs. Slime is going to be on standby, too, in case of an emergency. You remember she used

to be the McNastys' second mate? She hates the McNastys as much as we do. She still blames them for giving her an everlasting cold. Please, Mom, let us try. We know we can outwit the McNastys, and maybe this time they'll stay away from Little Snoring forever."

Mrs. Trout smiled and nodded. She knew how clever and brave Hetty and Tat were.

"And," said Mr. Trout, "I've got just the thing that might come in handy. A tube of my latest invention: Trout's Miracle Glue."

Mrs. Trout looked doubtful. "I do hope, my dear, that your miracle glue actually works, unlike Trout's Miracle Everlasting Ice, which melted in two seconds flat, and Trout's Miracle Everlasting Popping Corn, which popped so miraculously that it spilled over the top of the saucepan and filled the entire first floor of the house so we couldn't get in through the front door for two days."

Mr. Trout looked a little hurt at his wife's criticism.

"What's so miraculous about the glue?" asked Hetty.

"It's a glue and unglue in one handy tube. Apply it and it will stick anything to anything. Once it's dried completely you simply need to apply another dab and the things you've stuck together will miraculously unstick. Very useful if you've accidentally stuck the wrong things together, like that time your poor mother mistook superglue for lip salve and stuck her lips together."

Mrs. Trout shuddered at the memory.

"Does it actually work, Dad?" asked Tat.

"Ahem. Getting there," said Mr. Trout, a little sheepishly. "It definitely sticks things together superbly. But I haven't quite got the unsticking bit right yet. There's some vital ingredient missing. I'm just trying to work out what it is. At the moment, once stuck, it can only be unstuck after twenty-four hours using the specialist — and very expensive — methods currently employed in such situations, which would be unfortunate if you had accidentally superglued your bum to the toilet seat.

Can you spot some glue disasters on these pages? (No prizes.)

I can dribble but can't shoot!

But when I've discovered the secret ingredient, I think there will be a massive demand."

"Of course there will be," said Tallulah, rolling her eyes, "because people are always going around supergluing their bums to toilet seats."

"It happens more than you might think," said Mr. Trout. "But for the moment, you need to take care with the glue. Or you could find yourselves in a very sticky situation."

"We'll be careful," said Tat.

"We are used to sticky situations," said Hetty. And then she said thoughtfully, "Thanks for the glue, Mr. Trout, I think it could come in very useful."

Reward Offered

There were a great many excellent words on these two pages (in fact some of the best ones I have ever written). Unfortunately the glue used to stick them down was not Trout's Miracle Glue but a glue of very inferior quality, and the words have fallen off and rolled away on the floor. Some have been spotted being carried away by a family of hungry mutant zombie armadillos.

WORD

The police have advised that on no account should they be approached as they are armored and dangerous. But if by any chance you find any of the words lying about, please return them to this page immediately. They will be easy to identify as belonging to me as they all begin and end with a letter of the alphabet.

Chapter 6

The Little Snoring Café was unusually full.
Word had spread very quickly around the
village from Mrs. Groan's shop that Inspector
Haddock was about to make the imminent arrest
of the ghost of Captain Syd, and everybody
wanted to know more.

Mrs. Groan, whose shop was now closed for

the afternoon, was sitting in the corner, repeating everything that Inspector Haddock had told her.

"Such a clever man and apparently he can juggle, too."

"Ooh, what a talented policeman," said one of her friends. "I do hope Inspector Haddock makes an arrest soon. It's terrifying to think that the vengeful ghost of Captain Syd is on the loose. We might all be murdered in our beds."

"We might," said Mrs. Groan, looking rather thrilled at the prospect. "None of us are safe until an arrest has been made. I'm worried about all those children out in the dark at the Little Snoring Junior Costume Dance in the village hall when there is a murderous ghost on the loose."

She glanced at Hetty and Tat, who had come to the table to give her and her friends more scones and jam, and said, "I knew no good would come of all that digging for Captain Syd's lost treasure. Maybe it's you two who have brought the curse of Captain Syd down upon us all."

Hetty glanced over to the next table where

two strangers, a pair of very odd-looking and strangely hairy women, were sitting together with their heads lowered. Most people had taken no notice of them — they were far too keen to hear what Mrs. Groan had to say and discuss the latest developments among themselves — but Hetty had been keeping a sharp eye on them. They looked so peculiar.

She suddenly remembered the underpants stolen from the clothesline. Hetty smiled. She was pretty certain that she knew exactly who they were — the Ghastly McNastys! She nudged Tat, who glanced at the two strangers and gave Hetty a wink. Hetty knew that Tat guessed they were the McNastys, too.

"Oh," she said loudly and very casually, "I think Tat and I can look after ourselves."

"Yes," said Tat. "If those horrible, treasure-grabbing Ghastly McNastys, who are the kind of pirates who give pirates a bad name, don't frighten us, I don't think we're going to be worried by a ghost."

Everyone groaned and snarled at the mention of the Ghastly McNastys, and a few people, including Mrs. Groan — who had once been the Little Snoring featherweight boxing champion — even raised their fists.

The two strange, hairy women at the next table shifted uncomfortably, and if you had looked very carefully, you would have seen wisps of smoke coming out of their ears. But only Hetty and Tat noticed.

"First thing tomorrow we'll be digging down at the treasure site close to the abandoned graveyard by the cliffs at the point where the beach meets the Big, Scary, Very Dark, Dense Forest Where No One In Their Right Mind Would Want To Go, which had gotten BIGGER and SCARIER than it had been before.

"Of course, tonight we'll be at the Little Snoring Junior Costume Dance. We are confident that tomorrow is the day that we will find Captain Syd's lost treasure. All we've got to do is dig a little deeper and the treasure will be ours."

"If you don't get murdered by a ghost first," said Mrs. Groan, and she couldn't quite keep the excitement out of her voice.

"Good luck to you," said one of her friends. "You're braver than I am. I'm not always in my right mind but I wouldn't go close to the abandoned graveyard, by the cliffs, at the point where the beach meets the Big, Scary, Very Dark,

Dense Forest Where No One In Their Right Mind Would Want To Go, which had gotten BIGGER and SCARIER than it had been before, not for all the treasure in the world. Not with Captain Syd's ghost in a vengeful mood and already responsible for the disappearance of *The Good Hope.*"

"Me neither," agreed everyone in the café.

Unnoticed, except by Tat and Hetty, the two strangers got up and waddled out of the café in their ill-fitting skirts.

Outside, the McNastys grinned at each other, which was a horrible sight.

"Sweaty socks!" said Captain Gruesome. "Let's go to the treasure site and dig up the treasure!"

"Squeaky underpants! What a luscious idea! Let's go after dark when those horrible, revolting children will be at the Little Snoring Junior Costume Dance," said Captain Grisly.

For once the brothers agreed.

Another Very Important Warning Do Not Ignore

(even if you are busy juggling)

We have had reports that not everyone has heeded the warning at the beginning of this book. It is imperative that you do not leave this book unattended at any time. The publishers have (very wisely, in my pet terrapin's humble opinion) taken the precaution of sticking the McNastys to each page using Trout's Miracle Glue. But you can't be too careful. DO NOT LET THIS BOOK OUT OF YOUR SIGHT. Not even when you are asleep. YOU HAVE BEEN WARNED. The publishers cannot be held responsible if the McNastys escape from the pages and hold your hamster for ransom, cut off all your sister's hair and make her cry, steal your dad's piggy bank or eat all the chocolate cookies in the cookie jar, for which you will undoubtedly be blamed however much you protest your innocence.

P.S. If any of you see a ferret or any fleas or nits running around your bedroom, please stay exactly where you are and call for help. A ferret running around your bedroom always bodes ill, although it is not as scary as having rioting armored armadillos running around your bedroom.

Chapter 7

The McNastys thought they had disposed of Jamie Fried-Trout, but just as they were wrong about so many things, they were wrong about this. All Jamie's practice holding his breath underwater in the bath had paid off. He had managed to stay underwater for infinitely longer than the McNastys thought was possible, so they had departed to Little Snoring in their rowboat believing he was dead.

Kicking hard, Jamie shot up out of the water like a cork. Fortunately, he had surfaced quite close to *The Good Hope*. Unfortunately, he was not close enough to grab on to the rope ladder that hung tantalizingly close but just out of his grasp. His breath was coming in great gasps. But it wasn't going to do him much good, because he couldn't swim and, although he was only several feet from the rope ladder and safety, he could just as well have been a hundred miles away in Bigbottoms-by-the-Sea.

Jamie's cap is NOT stuck on with Trout's Miracle Glue, but fixed with excellent hairpins, as every young sailor knows.

He felt himself start sinking again. He floundered around kicking with his legs and flailing with his arms. But his panic was hindering rather than helping him. He took in a great gulp of seawater, which made him choke and splutter. He began to sink down into the water. He was going to drown. He could see his life flashing before him (which didn't take long as it had been so short) and it made him sad he would never do all the things he wanted to do, such as walk a tightrope across Niagara Falls, win the World Breath-Holding Championship and get first prize again for his costume at the annual Little Snoring Junior Costume Dance. His lungs hurt.

He became aware that something was nudging his bottom and pushing him upward. That something, he realized, was a nose. A shark's nose.

So now he was not just going to drown, he was going to be eaten, too! Life was so unfair!

But the shark just kept gently prodding him, and then suddenly he felt himself being wrapped in a long arm and he was raised up out of the water. He took a gulp of air. It was more delicious than strawberry ice cream.

For a moment he was held midair in the giant arm and then he was deposited on the deck of *The Good Hope*. He lay there gasping with shock for a few seconds and then he struggled up and peered over the side of the boat. Looking up at him were the shark (who he now recognized as the one he had helped to rid itself of the Ghastly McNastys) and the giant squid that they had so abused. The pair had saved him from drowning.

"Thank you! Thank you for saving me!" he called to them, and he bowed deeply to show his respect. The giant squid raised a tentacle and gave a bashful little wave.

"I'm going to thank you in the only way I can," said Jamie. "I'm going to find those nasty, ghastly twins and make sure they are brought to justice for hijacking *The Good Hope* and being horrible to sharks, squids and children."

The shark put its flippers together and the squid raised two of its arms out of the water and put them together, too. It was as if both creatures were clapping their approval.

Tat, Hetty, Dog, Polly and Mrs. Slime were hiding just inside the Big, Scary, Very Dark, Dense Forest Where No One In Their Right Mind Would Want To Go, which had gotten BIGGER and SCARIER than it had been before, in a spot from where they could keep a good watch on the site of their treasure dig without being seen.

It was not pleasant hiding there because the forest was not a pleasant place, and it never failed to live down to its name. Already they had had to rescue Dog from a mutant form of catnip, which when he had sniffed it had nipped his nose hard, and save Polly from a disagreeable bird-of-paradise that had tried to pinch her. Mrs. Slime was none too happy either, as the children had been worried that her sneezing might alert the McNastys, so she had been obliged to wear a clothespin on her nose. This was extremely uncomfortable as all of you will know from those occasions (family weddings, school assemblies) when it has been necessary to wear a clothespin on your nose.

Mrs. Slime was beginning to feel like a human volcano that was about to explode at any moment. There was a terrible pressure building up in her nose. She just hoped her nose wouldn't fall off when she did eventually sneeze as, despite her persistent cold, she had always considered her nose — which was neither too big nor too small — one of her best features. She was worried that her face would look very odd if her nose fell off. (Try drawing your own face without a nose and you will see that Mrs. Slime probably had a good point.)

Suddenly, they all spotted a light bobbing a little way offshore and heard the splash of oars.

"This could be them," said Tat.

Sure enough, a few minutes later, the McNastys appeared on the shore. They had changed out of the ladies' clothes and rowed around to the beach where Tat and Hetty were digging for treasure.

The children heard Gruesome tell his brother to put out his flashlight, but Grisly replied that there was no need. "If they see lights it will just make those silly superstitious villagers more scared and believe that the ghost of Captain Syd is on the rampage."

"Smart thinking," said Gruesome between gritted teeth, wishing that he had thought of it himself.

The Ghastly McNastys crept up the beach to the place by the cliffs where the sands met the Big, Scary, Very Dark, Dense Forest Where No One In Their Right Mind Would Want To Go, which had gotten BIGGER and SCARIER than it had been before.

They reached the big hole where Tat and Hetty had been digging for treasure and only just avoided falling into it. The hole was almost as big as a diplodocus, which is very big indeed.

The children had left two shovels lying by the top of the hole because they guessed, correctly, that the McNastys would have forgotten to bring their own.

The McNastys grabbed the shovels and climbed down the ladder into the hole and started digging greedily. They were sure that they would find the treasure very quickly.

They were so busy that they didn't notice that the children, Dog, Pegleg Polly and Mrs. Slime had all left their hiding places and had very quietly made their way over to the hole.

Very stealthily, the children pulled up the ladder. The McNastys were so keen to find the treasure that they didn't notice a thing.

Then Hetty got out the tube of Trout's Miracle Glue that Mr. Trout had given her and squeezed it out in a thick circle all around

the treasure hole. Careful to avoid stepping on the glue, they all crept back from the hole and watched with interest as the McNastys continued to dig, getting hotter and sweatier and more bad-tempered by the moment. The McNastys had taken off their shoes and socks so they could feel the cooling dirt between their toes.

"Goodness, that really does look like hard work," said Hetty very loudly, with a sweet smile.

"It does," agreed Tat. "I'm glad it's not us

doing all that heavy lifting. It's lovely to have someone else to do the digging. If they keep going, they should find the treasure for us very soon indeed. They've saved us getting all hot and bothered. So thank you."

The McNastys gave a squeal of fury and rushed toward the ladder. But the ladder was not there, and they just bumped their heads together very hard. When they recovered, they shook their fists at the children, Mrs. Slime, Dog and Polly, who all smiled back down at them very pleasantly.

"Let us out!" shouted the McNastys.

"Only if you tell us what you did with *The Good Hope* and all her crew," said Hetty.

"Never!" shouted the McNastys.

The children and Mrs. Slime stood up and started to stroll away.

"Wait!" shouted Captain Gruesome, thinking quickly, which sent shooting pains up and down his spine because he normally thought slower than a sloth. "Let us out of the hole, and we'll tell you."

He winked slyly at his brother. As soon as the children and Mrs. Slime put down the ladder and let them out, they would overpower them, force them down the hole and get them to do the digging for them.

"Do you promise?" asked Tat, who knew how much the McNastys' promises were worth, which was less than nothing plus nothing, which is more nothing than anyone knows what to do with.

"Of course we promise," said the McNastys with crocodile smiles. "We're even prepared to repent for all our ghastly nastiness in the past and promise that in the future we will give any treasure we steal … eh, sorry, find … to charity."

"Do we believe them?" Tat asked Hetty with a twinkle in his eye.

"Well, they are in a hole lot of trouble," said Hetty.

"Yes," agreed Mrs. Slime, "they have dug themselves deep."

"Pleeeeeeeeease," begged the McNastys, "we promise to be good as gold, and there's nothing gooder than gold."

"All right, we believe you," said Tat, but of course he didn't.

The children put down the ladder and wearily the McNastys began to climb it.

While they did, Tat scribbled a note to Inspector Haddock telling him to come to the beach and arrest the McNastys. Polly flew off with the note in her beak. Then the children, Mrs. Slime and Dog positioned themselves just outside the circle of glue as the McNastys emerged from the hole.

The McNastys waited until they were both on the surface and then they launched themselves at the children. They reached out their arms and hands to grab them. Gruesome had Tat by the shoulders and Grisly had Hetty. The children pulled themselves backward and both the McNastys toppled over from the knees. Their feet were stuck fast in Trout's Miracle Glue.

I have just received some very disturbing information. I hope you are sitting down, since you may faint when you hear this frightful news. Cheapskates as ever, the publishers refused to buy Trout's Miracle Glue and instead stuck the McNastys to each page in this book using glue bought on sale at the Bigbottoms-by-the-Sea flea market!

The almost total lack of stickiness means that there is a very real danger that on page 97, the McNastys will rise from the page and rampage around your house unless you keep a sharp eye on them and only ever read this book in a locked closet.

Chapter 8

The McNastys gave a howl of rage as they realized what had happened. They tried to pull their feet away, but their feet wouldn't budge. They snarled like angry armored armadillos when they realized that they had fallen into a trap.

"Let us out!" shouted the McNastys.

"Never," said Tat happily, thinking that it was probably easier to get the McNastys' cooperation by telling them that he wouldn't unstick them, rather than telling them that he couldn't unstick them and that they would have to wait twenty-four hours or until Mr. Trout had discovered the secret ingredient that would make Trout's Miracle Glue unstick. "I'm afraid we will not apply the unsticking solution until you've made a full confession of everything you've done, and signed it, too."

The McNastys keep evidence of their
favorite crimes in their photo album.

"Everything?" asked the McNastys, looking
worried. If they confessed all the nasty, ghastly
things they had done, they would be confessing
until next year, and they would also have to
admit that they were the nasty killjoys behind the
campaign to permanently cancel all birthdays for
children under the age of twelve.

"Just everything connected with the
disappearance of *The Good Hope*, for which we are
holding you responsible," said Hetty firmly.

"Guilty as charged!" said the McNastys proudly. "We hijacked the boat and we made all the crew walk the plank. Except that pesky little cabin boy. But we did him in, too, in the end. They're all fish food now."

Tat felt as if somebody had removed all the bones from his legs. He sank to the ground and put his head in his hands. His cousin Jamie was dead, and all the other crew members of *The Good Hope,* too. He felt terrible. They had all died because the McNastys were so greedy to get their hands on Captain Syd's lost treasure. He wished that he and Hetty had given up looking for the treasure. Maybe if they had, the Ghastly McNastys would have given up, too, and all the crew of *The Good Hope* would still be alive.

He walked away, and Hetty, seeing his distress, signaled to Mrs. Slime to stay and watch the McNastys, even though the McNastys were going nowhere very quickly. Their feet were quite stuck.

Hetty put her arm around Tat's shoulder, and Dog put a paw in Tat's hand.

Mrs. Slime kept a sharp eye on the McNastys (always better than keeping a blunt eye on someone).

"Is there really any treasure buried here?" asked Captain Gruesome. "Or was it just a sticky trick?"

Mrs. Slime took the clothespin off her nose because she couldn't answer with it there.

She nodded. "Oh, the children are really confident that they are very close. Just a few more feet of digging and they will have found the treasure." She smiled. "And you won't even get a glimpse of it because Inspector Haddock will have arrested you, and you will be locked up in the Little Snoring Jail where you will only have sadness and spiders for company. The inspector is on his way here now with his handcuffs."

Mrs. Slime felt an enormous sneeze coming on.

Her nose began to tingle dangerously. Her cold was always worse when she was stressed, and, apart from finding yourself in the middle of rioting mutant zombie armadillos, there was no greater stress in the world than finding yourself in close proximity to the McNastys. There was a noise like a thunderclap and she sneezed all over them.

ACHOO!

The children turned. Her snot poured all over the McNastys' feet … and the glue immediately came unstuck!

Mrs. Slime's snot was the vital missing secret ingredient for Trout's Miracle Glue (That You Can Unglue if You've Made a Terrible and Much Regretted Mistake with Your Gluing)!

But it was no moment for celebration, because immediately the McNastys threw a sack over Mrs. Slime, which made her fall over. The children and Dog raced back toward the pirates. Dog got there first, but Captain Gruesome grabbed Dog and held a knife to the poor cat's throat.

"One step farther, and the dratted dog — I mean mangy cat — gets it in the neck." He grinned. "I've always wanted to try cat burgers."

The children knew he wasn't joking. They put their hands up to show that they would offer no resistance, and Captain Grisly tied Hetty and Tat and Mrs. Slime's hands in front of them, tied Dog's front paws together and marched them down to the rowboat and forced them in at knifepoint.

Then the McNastys got in themselves and started to row away from the shore.

"This is going to be fun," said Gruesome.

"Where are you taking us?" demanded Tat.

The McNastys just grinned nastily as if they were enjoying a private joke.

"Listen!" said Hetty urgently. "You can have the treasure if you want it so badly. Just let us go, and it's all yours. We promise."

The McNastys cackled. They never kept any of their promises so they didn't believe anybody else's promises either.

"We're not stupid," said Gruesome. "We are going to dispose of you once and for all. We are going to rub you out."

Mrs. Slime began to cry quietly. She didn't want to be rubbed out — it sounded very painful.

Although Hetty felt quite like crying herself, she knew that crying was no help at all in their current dire situation.

"There is no room for melancholy in this boat," she said kindly but firmly.

Tat quickly glanced around the boat for Melancholy Smith. Then he realized his mistake — Hetty merely meant that being sad and crying wasn't going to help their situation.

The McNastys were finding rowing such a full boat very hard work, but the idea of ridding themselves of the children and their friends spurred them on.

"Where are we going?" demanded Hetty.

"You'll see soon enough," said Gruesome happily.

It was Tat who realized first, and it made his heart sink to his shoes. He spied the rocks that rose from the sea like vicious teeth, which were known locally as the Jaws and which many a boat and ship had floundered on until the building of the Little Snoring lighthouse. At low tide the rocks

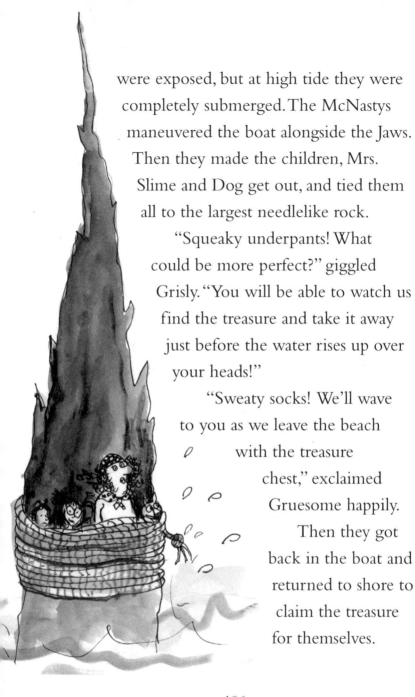

were exposed, but at high tide they were completely submerged. The McNastys maneuvered the boat alongside the Jaws. Then they made the children, Mrs. Slime and Dog get out, and tied them all to the largest needlelike rock.

"Squeaky underpants! What could be more perfect?" giggled Grisly. "You will be able to watch us find the treasure and take it away just before the water rises up over your heads!"

"Sweaty socks! We'll wave to you as we leave the beach with the treasure chest," exclaimed Gruesome happily. Then they got back in the boat and returned to shore to claim the treasure for themselves.

The children and the others stood forlornly on the Jaws.

"All right, Hetty, any bright ideas about how we escape?" asked Tat, trying to keep his voice cheerful and not show his fear.

Hetty shook her head sadly. Everyone always said that Hetty knew everything. But she didn't have a clue how they were going to escape from the Jaws.

"Too bad," said Tat stoically, "because the tide seems to be rising very fast indeed."

(There was a lovely picture of Tat, Hetty, Mrs. Slime and Dog on this page, but regrettably it had been drawn in pencil and my terrapin came along with an eraser and they have all been rubbed out, which is very sad and made me cry.)

Chapter 9

Polly landed on the front desk of the police station. The desk sergeant looked at the front of the note, which was addressed to Inspector Gullible Haddock. Hetty and Tat didn't have much confidence in Inspector Haddock's abilities to solve crimes, but he was a policeman so they were certain he would want to come to the beach and arrest the McNastys, who were always at the top of Little Snoring's most-wanted list.

"I'm afraid the inspector is busy juggling at the moment — he can't be disturbed," the desk sergeant said.

Polly pushed the note toward the sergeant, who opened it. He could immediately see how urgent it was. The Little Snoring police force had been trying to catch the Ghastly McNastys for years.

He ran into the back room where the inspector was trying and failing to juggle six balls.

"Sir, we've had an urgent message sent by parrot post from two children called Tat and Hetty. It says that if you go down to the beach and the place by the cliffs near the Big, Scary, Very Dark, Dense Forest Where No One In Their Right Mind Would Want To Go, which had gotten BIGGER and SCARIER than it had been before, you will be able to solve the disappearance of *The Good Hope* and arrest the Ghastly McNastys."

"Go away!" shouted Inspector Haddock. "I've already solved the disappearance of *The Good Hope*. The Ghastly McNastys are no longer at the top of Little Snoring's most-wanted list. Besides, those f lea- and ferret-infested varmints are miles away inside a shark. I am busy juggling and trying to work out how I'm going to arrest a ghost. I fear that dratted but undeniably clever Hetty may have a point — it is going to be very hard to put handcuffs on a specter. But I will use my oversized brain to solve the problem. And I will succeed. Otherwise everyone will say I'm just a big head."

"More of a nitwit," muttered the policeman to himself as he walked away. "Sorry," he said to Polly. "That inspector is a bit of a birdbrain."

The sergeant blushed. "My apologies. I didn't mean to be rude."

Polly didn't mind. She knew she was smarter than Inspector Haddock and she flew away in search of Mrs. Trout.

Jamie Fried-Trout was rowing across the sea toward Little Snoring. He had been so exhausted after landing back onto *The Good Hope* that he had fallen asleep, and by the time he woke up, it was dark. The moon had come out and was shining as brightly as it could to help Jamie on his way. If Jamie was going to get revenge upon the McNastys, the moon was determined to do anything that it could to help. It didn't take kindly to being hit by dried snot pellets from the McNastys' catapults.

Jamie had changed
into his costume —
the ghost of Captain
Syd — and planned to
give Tat and Hetty
an enormous
surprise when
he turned up
unannounced at the
Little Snoring Junior
Costume Dance. He hoped he might give them a
bit of a fright, and of course he would be able to
tell everyone that the rest of the crew from *The
Good Hope* were alive and well and simply needed
rescuing from the island where the shark had taken
them.

He rowed hard, humming
quietly to himself, when he thought
he heard someone shouting "Help!"
In fact, he thought it was more than
one person shouting "Help!" Where
was it coming from?

Help!

He could see the vicious rocks known as the Jaws rising from the sea. He knew that he should keep a safe distance from them because many a ship and boat had been wrecked on their needle-sharp teeth that were hidden underneath the water at high tide.

There was no mistaking it. Somebody was in trouble on the far side of the Jaws.

Help!

"Help!"

If he wasn't mistaken, there were several people and they appeared to have a cat with them, or maybe it was a dog. It was hard to tell. There also seemed to be quite a lot of sneezing.

Jamie began rowing as fast as he could around the side of the Jaws but taking great care not to get too close.

The sea was rising fast. It was now up to the children's chests and Mrs. Slime's waist. They had all frantically been trying to loosen the ropes that bound their hands together and held them fast against the rocks. But the water had made the knots harder to undo.

"There is no hope," wailed Mrs. Slime. Stress had made her sneeze continuously so that the sea surrounding the Jaws had become quite snotty and the tide of goo from her nose was only adding to the rising sea level. "We are in the jaws of death," she wailed, and nobody contradicted her because it was quite true.

"It's not over until it's over," said Hetty firmly.

"We are up to our necks in it, Hetty," said Tat.

"Actually, Tat, the water hasn't quite reached our necks," said Hetty, who, even when she was staring death in the face, was a stickler for accuracy.

Tat said nothing as it was quite clear that it was going to be over sooner than any of them would have wished. He thought he heard the sound of an oar against water. Maybe the McNastys had had a change of heart? (This doesn't mean that they had swapped hearts with somebody else, but that they had suddenly become nicer and kinder, which of course is very unlikely, and had changed their minds.) Maybe Inspector Gullible Haddock had come to their rescue? Or maybe the imminence of death was simply making him delirious so he thought he was hearing things.

"Help!" Tat shouted, but rather more faintly.

There was no answering cry, but suddenly a rowboat loomed around the side of the Jaws and headed toward them.

"Oh, fishcakes," moaned Mrs. Slime between sneezes, spotting the boat and its occupant. "We're not going to drown after all, but we are going to be murdered by the vengeful ghost of Captain Syd."

"That's not Captain Syd!" shouted Tat. "That's my cousin Jamie in his costume, I think."

He paused. "Are you a ghost, Jamie? Did you drown and come back to haunt us?"

"Of course he isn't a ghost," said Hetty.

"Hetty's right," said Jamie, as he very carefully lined the boat up beside the Jaws, leaped on the rocks and proceeded to untie them.

"Hetty is almost always right," said Tat.

"I told you it wasn't over," said Hetty, looking quite pleased with herself.

"It won't be over until we've gotten rid of the Ghastly McNastys," said Jamie. "And who knows, if we hurry, maybe we'll even get to the Little Snoring Junior Costume Dance before that's over, too."

Chapter 10

M rs. Trout was worried in the way only a
mother can be, and Polly was making her
more anxious flying round and round her head
and clearly trying to tell her something.

"Nasty boys, porky pies," she kept squawking,
and Mrs. Trout knew that Polly was referring to
the McNastys.

Mrs. Trout had every faith in Tat and Hetty, and knew that they were more than a match for the McNastys, but she had been expecting them home to change into their costumes, and they hadn't turned up.

So she set off following Polly, who led her to the police station.

"Oh, it's you again," said the sergeant when he saw Polly. "You know I did my best to get Inspector Haddock to act on the note, but he refused even to read it."

"Let me see the note," said Mrs. Trout, and she sounded so angry that the sergeant handed it over without a squeak.

"Good girl, Polly," said Mrs. Trout when she had read it, and she pushed the desk sergeant aside and strode into the back room.

"You can't go in there . . ." he began.

But she had. She found Inspector Gullible Haddock standing in the middle of the room trying to Hula-Hoop very badly.

Mrs. Trout was furious.

It wasn't the inspector's dismal incompetence at the Hula-Hoop that made Mrs. Trout so angry (although he clearly had absolutely no talent for it at all and was wasting his and the Hula-Hoop's time) but the fact that Tat, Hetty, Dog and Mrs. Slime were facing the Ghastly McNastys all alone.

She was as angry as a lioness who realizes that her cubs are being threatened. She marched right up to Inspector Haddock, who dropped his Hula-Hoop in surprise.

"Why did you ignore the message from Tat and Hetty about the Ghastly McNastys being down on the beach?" she demanded.

Inspector Haddock gave a snooty smile. "I ignored it because I have already solved the case of *The Good Hope*. In this instance the Ghastly McNastys are innocent."

"The Ghastly McNastys are never innocent," roared Mrs. Trout, "and I've heard your theory about the ghost of Captain Syd being responsible for the disappearance of *The Good Hope,* and it's complete nonsense. At this very moment two children, a cat and a lady with a very persistent cold who should be tucked up warm in bed with a hot water bottle are facing up to the McNastys all on their own while you fiddle around learning circus skills and trying to dream up ways to arrest a ghost that doesn't even exist."

She put her face very close to Inspector Haddock's face. "Do you know what you are?"

"The world's greatest detective?" mumbled Inspector Haddock more in hope than expectation.

"You are a complete clown!" said Mrs. Trout, and all the rest of the Little Snoring police force, who had been listening just outside the door, broke into loud laughter. "And you are coming with me to find out what's happened to those brave children and to arrest the Ghastly McNastys." She turned to the rest of the Little Snoring police force. "And you'd better all come, too. Things may get very nasty and ghastly."

At the same time as Mrs. Trout arrived at the police station, the children, Dog and Mrs. Slime arrived at the Trout family home. Tat and Hetty changed into their skeleton costumes. They added a few pirate touches such as eye-patches and hats. They even found skeleton costumes for Mrs. Slime and Dog.

Then they took full cans of glow-in-the-dark paint and all the remaining supplies of Trout's Miracle Glue from the garden shed and hurried down the path toward the beach where they had left the rowboat.

With Tat and Jamie rowing as hard and fast as they could, they soon arrived at the secluded cove where *The Good Hope* was moored. Mrs. Slime and Jamie quickly got to work hoisting the mast back in place and securing it with Trout's Miracle Glue. "Just make sure you don't sneeze over it," Tat told Mrs. Slime.

Meanwhile the others started painting the ship all over with glow-in-the-dark paint. Very conveniently, at that moment, Polly, who had been flying around the island looking for them, arrived and proved very helpful with a paintbrush.

She flew around the outside of the ship in record time and daubed it in a thick layer of paint.

"Now all we need is for the moon to shine very brightly so the paint really glows, and then have the moon disappear behind a cloud at exactly the right moment," said Hetty. "Goodness," she said, looking up to the sky, which had suddenly become enormously bright, "it's almost as if the moon heard me." She gave a little laugh. "But of course that's impossible. It would be like believing in ghosts."

At the treasure site, the McNastys were feeling more than a little spooked. They knew that they, not the ghost of Captain Syd, were responsible for the disappearance of *The Good Hope*, but that didn't stop them worrying that he might take his revenge on them when they found the treasure.

They jumped at the smallest sound. At one point an owl had hooted, and they had both tried to jump into the other's arms and instead had ended up on the ground.

They were also uncomfortably hot again. They had been digging for ages and there was still no sign of the treasure. They were beginning to think that they had been tricked again, and they would have rowed back out to the Jaws to punch the children very hard if it was not for the fact that climbing up the ladder was hard work. They were also eager to find the treasure quickly so that Tat, Hetty and the others would see them with the treasure chest before drowning. As they were down in the hole digging, they hadn't seen Jamie rescue the children.

The McNastys were rather regretting that they hadn't gotten the children and Mrs. Slime to do the digging for them and then buried them alive in the hole once they had found the treasure. Each of the McNastys blamed the other for not thinking of that.

"What we need is a helping hand," said Gruesome.

"Nobody ever wants to help us," said Grisly mournfully.

"Maybe we can entice some children away from the Little Snoring Junior Costume Dance and force them to dig for us," mused Gruesome.

Suddenly, Grisly smiled a cunning smile. "I've got a much better idea that will go out with a bang." And he climbed up the ladder, ran down to the rowboat and found the six sticks of dynamite, some fuse wire and a box of matches that he had brought from the ship. He was so excited that he didn't notice the children were no longer tied to the Jaws. "We'll blast our way to the treasure!"

Gruesome sniffed. He didn't want to show his brother that he was impressed by his smart thinking, but he thought it was the best idea that

Grisly had ever had. Even better than the time that he had stolen all the ice creams from the children on the beach at Bigbottoms-by-the-Sea.

Very quickly, the pirates laid the dynamite and then they ran a fuse until they judged that they were far enough away to be quite safe.

They were just about to light it when they heard shouting from the top of the beach.

Racing toward them was the entire Little Snoring police force, led by Inspector Haddock. The police all had their handcuffs at the ready. Following them was Mrs. Trout, who was waving her umbrella, and quite honestly she was the scariest sight of all (even more scary than a rioting armored armadillo or the vengeful ghost of Captain Syd).

She was yelling, "What have you done with my Tat and his friend Hetty? I'll have your guts for garters if you've touched a hair on their heads."

The McNastys looked at each other. They knew they ought to run, but the lure of the treasure was too great. They nodded at each other and then they both struck a match and lit the fuse. A river of

sparks ran along the fuse and down into the hole.

Inspector Gullible Haddock had just seized both McNastys by the scruff of the neck when there was an enormous explosion. The whole beach seemed to shudder as if it had been hit by a massive earthquake, and everyone was swept off their feet.

There was a terrible silence on the beach. The McNastys were the first to recover. They rushed to the edge of the hole and peered into it. They spied TREASURE!

The McNastys were so thrilled that they screamed with delight, a noise so horrible it was like the sound of forty jet airplanes landing just outside your bedroom window.

They stretched out their arms toward the treasure — and at that very moment there was another sound as if the earth itself was cracking in two, and the cliffs by the treasure site developed hundreds of fissures and fractures as a result of the McNastys' screams.

There was a moment when it seemed as if time stood still. And then, as if in slow motion, the front part of the cliffs tumbled down toward the treasure site. The McNastys only just jumped out of the way before thousands of tons of rock fell into the hole and covered it over completely. For a second everyone stood there completely stunned.

Then the McNastys burst into tears and began scrabbling at the huge rocks with their hands.

But it was useless. The treasure was buried, almost certainly forever.

The smoke and debris began to clear, and

when the McNastys, no longer blinded by the dazzle of the treasure, looked at what remained of the cliff, they saw a truly terrible and fearsome sight — a huge and ferocious skeleton monster was looming over them.

In their confusion and dazed state, the McNastys decided that it must be a ghost that had come to get them. They gave a scream of fright and began to run toward their rowboat at the edge of the sea.

But just as they reached it, they saw a huge ghostly pirate ship coming toward them. The entire ship was emitting an eerie green glow including the skull and crossbones that Jamie had taken from his pocket and that now flew from the top of the (slightly wonky) mast.

And worst of all, as far
as the Ghastly McNastys
were concerned, leering
at them from the prow of
the ship and shaking his cutlass at
them was unmistakably the ghost
of Captain Syd.

It was ten times more
frightening than anything they
had ever seen before, and it
was accompanied by a host
of pirate skeletons that were all pointing their
bony fingers at the McNastys, like fingers
of judgment.

"I'm coming to get you nasty pirates,"
roared Captain Syd, and the ship plowed its way
toward them and appeared to be about to run
straight onto the beach and the place where they
were standing.

The McNastys whimpered and shrieked.
They didn't know which way to turn. They were
caught between the ghost on the cliffs and the

specter of Captain Syd and his eerie glowing pirate ship in the water, and the Little Snoring police force and Mrs. Trout who were bearing down on them from the left.

The McNastys decided to run to the right. They ran along the beach as fast and as far away from the ship as they could and they then plunged into the sea, completely forgetting that neither of them could really swim very well.

They took several strokes and were carried by the retreating tide farther out to sea. They tried to take another stroke and instead swallowed great gulps of water. They spluttered and were about to sink, when a huge tentacle emerged from the ocean and curled around them both. They screamed and they shrieked as the giant squid swam off holding them tightly. Their shrieks and screams grew fainter and fainter.

As soon as they disappeared over the horizon, Tat, Hetty, Jamie and the others put down the anchor, climbed down the side of the ship, got into the rowboat and came ashore.

"Calm down, Mom, we're safe," said Tat happily as Mrs. Trout hugged him, Jamie and Hetty.

The children and Mrs. Slime explained to Mrs. Trout and Inspector Haddock everything that had happened and how the McNastys had admitted that they had been responsible for the disappearance of *The Good Hope.* Jamie also explained to the coast guard, who had been summoned by the police, the location where the crew of *The Good Hope* were stranded. He had spotted them just before hearing the cries for help on the Jaws. A boat was sent to rescue them immediately.

"Well," said Mrs. Trout, "I'm sorry that after all your hard work, Captain Syd's treasure is buried and probably lost forever. But it's been more trouble than it's worth, and I'm just pleased that you are all safe and sound. It's a pity that Inspector Haddock didn't get to arrest the Ghastly McNastys so we were rid of them once and for all."

"He can always arrest me as the ghost of Captain Syd!" piped up Jamie with a wicked smile.

Inspector Haddock turned scarlet and crept

away feeling completely humiliated. He vowed to give up being a detective; he felt that maybe clowning was his true vocation.

"Of course," said Hetty, "we may not have uncovered the treasure but we have discovered something very valuable." She pointed at the cliff. "I'm pretty sure that is the first time that the complete skeleton of a diplodocus has been discovered. I rather think that the dinosaur professors are going to be very interested."

"Dog! Put that bone down," shouted Tat, seeing Dog attempt to put a twenty-five-foot diplodocus bone in his mouth. "You can't eat that. It's 150 million years old. It will be moldier than most of the food in Mrs. Groan's shop. We'll get you a nice fresh bone from the butcher."

Dog obediently did as he was told and bounded over to lick Tat's face.

Chapter 11

Tat, Hetty and Jamie left the village hall and sat outside on the steps overlooking the sea, eating their bowls of ice cream. The Little Snoring Junior Costume Dance was still in full swing. Even though they had arrived late, it had been a lovely evening. Jamie's ghost of Captain Syd costume had been a big hit, and once again he'd won first prize.

Mr. Trout had been delighted to hear that Mrs. Slime's snot was the secret ingredient for Trout's Miracle Glue and was convinced that his invention would have a bright commercial future. It had already come in handy half an hour earlier when Melancholy Smith's elder sister stuck her to the village hall toilet seat after Melancholy beat her by winning second prize in the costume competition.

"See," said Mr. Trout, "it's always happening. There will be a massive demand for Trout's Miracle Glue."

The coast guard had turned up with the crew of *The Good Hope* just as the pizza and strawberry ice cream were being served, which was lucky since they were very hungry because they had been living on berries and coconuts for the last few days. The captain had been delighted to hear that her boat was intact thanks to Jamie and the others, even if it was covered in green glow-in-the-dark paint and the mast was a bit wobbly.

The last few days had seemed like a nightmare that was all over now. There had also been a call from Greater Snoring University. The world-famous dinosaur expert, Professor Dino Fossil, would be at the cliffs at first light and was very excited about the find.

Why are bad dreams called nightmares? Why not nightstallions?

The children finished their ice cream and wandered onto the beach. It was a brilliantly bright moonlit night, as if the moon had decided it had something to celebrate.

"Tat," asked Jamie, "do you mind that Captain Syd's lost treasure is probably buried forever after that landslide?"

Tat shook his head. "Not really. A diplodocus is much more exciting."

"At least the McNastys are out of our hair," said Hetty (who didn't mean that the McNastys had been living on her and Tat's heads but that they had been a great nuisance). "From what you tell us, Jamie, I bet that giant squid means business."

Jamie nodded.

"Yes," said Tat, "maybe we shouldn't press our luck and we should give up treasure hunting."

"It's not over until it's over," said a quiet voice behind them.

The children spun around. An elderly pirate was standing there. He wasn't threatening or vengeful at all and he had a twinkle in his eye and he looked very, very familiar, from pictures they had all seen in books.

"Captain Syd . . .?" asked Tat with wonder in his voice.

The pirate smiled and tipped his hat at them and winked, and as he did so he began to disappear.

Eventually all that was left of him was his smile hanging in the air, and then that also vanished.

"Hetty," said Tat firmly, "I know you don't believe in them, but I've definitely, maybe just seen a ghost."

"Me, too," said Hetty. "Definitely. Maybe."

Set sail on the first
GHASTLY McNASTYS adventure!

THE LOST TREASURE OF LITTLE SNORING

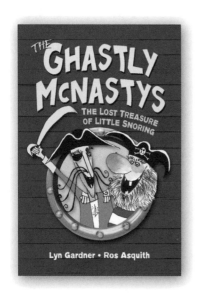

The Ghastly McNastys are the ghastliest, nastiest pirates ever to sail the seven seas. But on their endless quest for treasure, they come across Tat and Hetty — two local children who aren't going to let some thieving pirates get in their way.

"A laugh-out-loud offering for kids who enjoy over-the-top, goofy antics." — *School Library Journal*

Don't miss the second
dastardly delightful read!

RAIDERS OF THE LOST SHARK

The whole village is
excited when a film crew
comes to Little Snoring —
and none more so than
the Ghastly McNastys.
They plan to storm the
set as extras, steal Captain
Syd's treasure and show
everyone what being a
pirate really means!

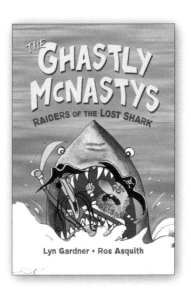

Only Tat and Hetty can see what the pirate twins
are really up to — but will anyone believe them?

Lyn Gardner is a theater critic for the *Guardian* and goes to the theater five or six times a week, which should leave no time for writing books. But actually she has written several children's books, including the very successful Stage School series. She lives in London, England.

Ros Asquith is a cartoonist for the *Guardian* and has written and illustrated many books. *Letters from an Alien Schoolboy* was shortlisted for the Roald Dahl Funny Prize, and *The Great Big Book of Families*, which she illustrated, won the SLA Information Book Award. She lives in London, England.